McDUFF STORIES

This book belongs to:

_____

First paper-over-boards edition, 2005
1 3 5 7 9 10 8 6 4 2

This book is set in Cochin.
Reinforced binding

ISBN 0-7868-5676-9
Library of Congress Cataloging-in-Publication Data on file.

Visit www.hyperionbooksforchildren.com

McDUFF
GOES TO SCHOOL

ROSEMARY WELLS • SUSAN JEFFERS

HYPERION BOOKS FOR CHILDREN

NEW YORK

A new name was painted on the mailbox at number nine Elm Road.
Marie-Antoinette sat among the movers' boxes.
She kept her eye on McDuff.

"Woof!" said McDuff.
"*Ouf,*" said Marie.

McDuff fidgeted up and down on his side of the fence.
Marie watched every move McDuff made,
but she did not leave her new porch.
"Viens Marie!" called a voice, and Marie trotted inside.

Lucy and Fred came out to see what was happening.
"They're speaking in a foreign language," said Fred.
"They are going to have to learn English."

Lucy brought a peach cobbler over to the de Gaulles.
Fred brought a pitcher of lemonade, and a Vita-Biskit for Marie.

"Hello!" said Lucy.

"Welcome to Elm Road," said Fred. "This is our dog, McDuff."

"*Bonjour!*" said Celeste de Gaulle.

"*C'est notre chienne, Marie,*" said Pierre.

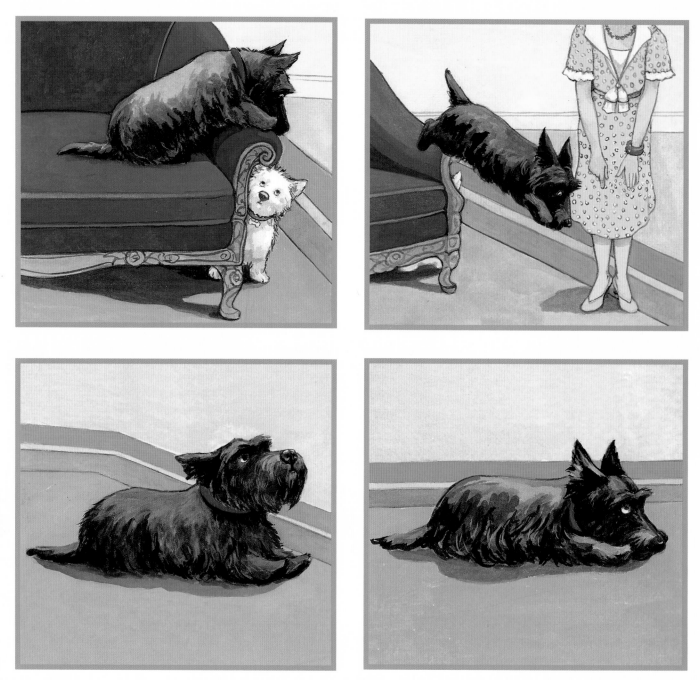

Celeste did not want Marie to sit on her sofa.
"*À bas!*" said Celeste. Marie jumped down.
"*Couche-toi!*" said Celeste. Marie lay down at Celeste's feet.
"*Reste-là, Marie!*" said Celeste. Marie stayed.

McDuff jumped onto the de Gaulles' sofa. Marie did not like it.
"Get down, McDuff!" said Lucy. McDuff did not get down.
"Come here, McDuff!" said Fred. McDuff sank deep into the sofa.
"He needs to go to school!" said Fred.

Celeste and Marie decided to go to school, too.

"Everyone here will soon heel, sit, stay, and come," said the trainer.
"Everyone must practice every day.
The best one will win a blue ribbon at graduation."

But Lucy was too busy with the baby to practice with McDuff.

And Fred was too tired after a day's work to practice with McDuff.

But every day Celeste practiced with Marie.
"Assieds-toi!" said Celeste, and Marie sat.

"*Au pied!*" said Celeste, and Marie walked at Celeste's heel.
"*Saute!*" said Celeste, and Marie jumped up to get a liver truffle.

"Woof!" said McDuff.
"Assieds-toi!" said Celeste.
McDuff sat. Celeste pushed a liver truffle through the fence.

Marie performed *assieds-toi, couche-toi,* and *au pied* perfectly.
Very soon McDuff did too.

"McDuff is not doing well," said the trainer.
"He doesn't understand *down, stay,* or *come.*
He may have D.A.I., Dog Attention-itis."
"It can't be him," said Fred. "It must be us."

On graduation day Lucy lined McDuff up with the other dogs.
"Sit!" said Lucy. But she had to push him down.

"Stay!" said Lucy. But McDuff ran to Fred.
"Disqualified!" said the judge.

All the dogs did their best *heel*s, *sit*s, and *stay*s.
Marie did figure eights, went over the hurdles, and retrieved
the correct rubber toy, all off-leash. She won the blue ribbon.

Celeste saw Lucy's and Fred's unhappy faces.
"Viens!" shouted Celeste.
McDuff raced across the lawn to Celeste.

"Assieds-toi!" said Celeste. McDuff sat perfectly square.
"Au pied!" said Celeste, and McDuff followed her step for step.
"Couche-toi! Reste-là!" said Celeste, and McDuff sank to the ground and did not move a hair. The judge gave McDuff a red ribbon.

Celeste made a grand French picnic
to celebrate the two winners.
"Viens!" said Lucy.
"Assieds-toi! Reste-là!" said Fred.
"Ouf!" said McDuff.

Glossary

à bas [ah-BAH]: get down

assieds-toi [ah-syeh-TWAH]: sit

au pied [oh-PYEH]: heel

couche-toi [koosh-TWAH]: lie down

saute [sohte]: jump

reste-là [rest-LAH]: stay

viens [vyehn]: come